Miss Pinkeltink's Purse

Tilbury House Publishers

12 Starr Street • Thomaston, Maine 04861

800-582-1899 • www.tilburyhouse.com

Text © 2018 by Patty Brozo

Illustrations © 2018 by Ana Ochoa

Hardcover ISBN 978-0-88448-626-8

eBook ISBN 978-0-88448-628-2

First hardcover printing October 2018

15 16 17 18 19 20 XXX 10 9 8 7 6 5 4 3 2 1

Library of Congress Control Number: 2018949275

Designed by Frame25 Productions

Printed in Korea through Four Colour Print Group

Miss Pinkeltink's Purse

written by PATTY BROZO

illustrated by ANA OCHOA

TILBURY HOUSE PUBLISHERS, THOMASTON, MAINE

Rosy-cheeked and quite antique, Miss Pinkeltink
carried everything but the kitchen sink.

From the day that she and her purse hit town,
what got in her way was what got knocked down.

The purse was so big that it dragged on the floor.
When she rode on the bus it got stuck in the door.

She plowed down the flowers in Veda's rose bed,
bumping a hoe that hit Sam in the head.

She knocked down Fred's fence and the box for his mail,
then set her purse down on his cockapoo's tail.

She created a stir when she strolled down Main Street,
bumping Zoey off her bike and Zach off his feet.

Some people in Bedford (as you may have guessed)
thought the purse and its owner *both* were a pest.

Miss Pinkeltink knew her huge purse was to blame,
so she gathered her courage and tried to explain:

"Sometimes it's a blessing, sometimes it's a curse,
but all that I have, I have in my purse."

Most people in Bedford didn't have to think twice.
They could see right away that the lady was nice.

When Miss Pinkeltink saw from the bench where she sat
that Zoey was crying—her bike had a flat—

the old woman pushed back her tattered pink cape,
reached into her purse and pulled out—some tape.

Then Zach needed help. His car wouldn't start.
He had the right tools, but he needed a part.

As Zach and his friends watched with hope and with wonder,
she dove into her purse and came up with—a plunger.

She gave Nicki a rake and Donald a comb.
She gave Veda's white kitty-cat, Phoebe, a bone.

Miss Pinkeltink's gifts never quite hit the mark,
but she gave what she had, and she gave from the heart.

Then Miss Pinkeltink looked in her purse in dismay.
It was empty! She'd given her treasures away.

But she took one more look in her bag's deepest folds,
and found something there a mere purse couldn't hold.

She saw all the pleasure her gifts could provide,
and it gave her a *wonderful* feeling inside.

She slept all that night underneath the big willow,
with her cape as a blanket, her purse as a pillow.

Looking into the night through her room's windowpane,
Zoey saw Miss Pinkeltink in the rain.

And she thought to herself, *Who sleeps in a park?*
Why sleep all alone where it's cold, wet, and dark?

She pictured the tape for the flat on her bike—
the tape she'd been given to make it all right.

Then a super idea popped into her mind.
We must do something special for someone so kind.

Zoey phoned all her friends and told them her scheme,
and they all got on board and worked as a team.

They called up their neighbors, each woman and man.
They told *everyone* about Zoey's great plan.

to call:
• Donald
• zach
• Veda
• Steve
• Fred
• Sam
• Nicki
• Bobby
• Lucy
• Rick
• Mary

Miss Pinkeltink slept on her tree-sheltered bed
as the willow's green leaves turned to gold, then to red.

One night it grew cold and the dew soaked her clothes,
then the frost settled down on her cheeks and her nose.

She shivered and dreamed of a fluffy, warm quilt
on her bed in the house that her father had built.

When the old woman woke up the following day,
she thought a parade must be coming her way.

All the people from town carried boxes and gifts,
and they led her up Main on a mystery trip.

Said Veda, "I know just what your purse needs."
And she gave her a packet of cucumber seeds.

"Your purse needs a toaster," said Zach with a wink.
"Your purse needs a blanket, some sheets, and a sink."

Said Nicki, "I think that your purse needs a bed."
"And a couch, and a table and chairs," added Fred.

They stopped on a lawn after walking a while,
and they faced the old woman, each wearing a smile.

"Your purse needs a stove." "Your purse needs a phone."
Then they all stepped aside. "And your purse needs a home!"

Homelessness

Being homeless means not having a place to live or sleep or keep belongings. Life is very hard for someone who is homeless.

Do you see homeless people in the town where you live? There are ways to help, just as Zoey did. Here are some other ways kids have helped:

www.ladybugfoundation.ca

Hannah Taylor was five years old when she saw a homeless man picking through the garbage on a cold day in winter. She founded The Ladybug Foundation, a charity for feeding and housing the homeless that is based in Winnipeg, Manitoba.

www.shelteringbooks.org

Mackenzie Bearup was 13 when she started collecting books for her local homeless shelter. Her charity, Sheltering Books, collected 460,000 books for shelters across the country by 2015.

loveinthemirror.org

Jonas Corona was only six when he visited homeless shelters with his mom and then founded Love in the Mirror. His mission is to inspire young people to make a difference through their volunteer commitment to helping the disadvantaged.

carebags4kids.com

Eleven-year-old Annie Wingall founded Care Bags 4 Kids to provide essential items to needy children around the world.

austingutwein.com

Hoops of Hope, founded by nine-year-old Austin Gutwein, hosts a yearly shoot-a-thon (basketball free throws) to provide orphans of AIDS victims with food, shelter, and other necessities. The organization has raised $2.5 million as of 2018.

If you want to help the homeless in your community, talk to your parents, caregiver, or teacher. Together you can come up with ways to help. Here are a few ideas:

* Stage a play, talent show, bake sale, or lemonade stand to raise money for a local shelter.

* On your next birthday, ask friends and relatives to bring a donation of food for a food pantry rather than a gift for you.

* Ask your parents to volunteer with you in a soup kitchen on Thanksgiving or any other day.

* Plant a garden and take your ripe vegetables to a food pantry.

Nobody is too small to do something BIG!

PATTY BROZO has been writing stories for and about children since taking creative writing classes in college. This is her first published work.

ANA OCHOA lives in Mexico and learned the art of children's book illustration from M. Claude Lapointe at L'Ecole Superieure des Arts Decoratifs in France. Her illustrations for *Storms in a Bottled Sea* were selected for the Illustrators Exhibition in Bologna in 1997. Her work has been exhibited in Japan, Taiwan, New Delhi, Bratislava, Brazil, Colombia, and Mexico. She has worked for major publishing houses in Mexico, Spain, and the United States. Her book *The Chocolate Boy*—with its main character a little Haitian boy who is subjected to discrimination and ignorance in a foreign land—was published in 2010 by the United Nations High Commissioner for Refugees (UNHCR).

Related Titles

Lailah's Lunchbox:
A Ramadan Story

978-0-88448-431-8

by Reem Faruqi, illustrated
by Lea Lyon

Say Something

978-0-88448-360-1

by Peggy Moss, illustrated
by Lea Lyon

Most People

978-0-88448-554-4

by Michael Leannah,
illustrated by
Jennifer E. Morris

The Lemonade Hurricane
A Story of Mindfulness
and Meditation

978-0-88448-396-0

by Licia Morelli, illustrated
by Jennifer E. Morris